BIZZ BUZZ BOSS

Written by Natalie McKinnon

Illustrated by Margaret Tolland

In a quiet corner of a quiet garden
lived a shy and gentle spider.
Homely sounds surrounded Little Spider as
she lay smiling in her cozy, curly leaf.

Day after day, she listened
to the peaceful garden song.
Drip, drip, drippety-drip came the
sound of the garden tap.
Swish, swish, swishety-swoosh
came the sound of the
leaves along the path.
Twit-twoo, twit-twoo came the
sound of the owl family
high in the tree.

But another sound also hummed
through the air.
Bizzz, buzzz, boss-boss-boss.

It was the sound of the bossiest
creature in the garden.
Every day Bossy Bee would
boss-boss-boss everyone else.
She thought she was the most
important creature in the garden.

When the shy worm wiggled towards
her, Bossy Bee flew away.
Bizzz, buzzz, boss-boss-boss.

"Go away, little worm. You're
wasting my time.
My work is important you see.
I collect pollen to take to my hive.
No one works as hard as me."

When the cheerful ladybug fluttered by,
Bossy Bee turned away.
Bizzz, buzzz, boss-boss-boss.

"Go away, ladybug. You're wasting my time.
My work is important you see.
I leave some pollen on every flower I visit.
No one works as hard as me."

Even when the happy lizard came to visit,
Bossy Bee turned away.
Bizzz, buzzz, boss-boss-boss.

"Go away, lazy lizard. You're wasting my time.
My work is important you see.
The pollen I leave on the flowers helps fruit grow.
No one works as hard as me."

The other garden creatures were tired of being bossed about by Bossy Bee.
They went to see the Little Spider, to ask her for advice.

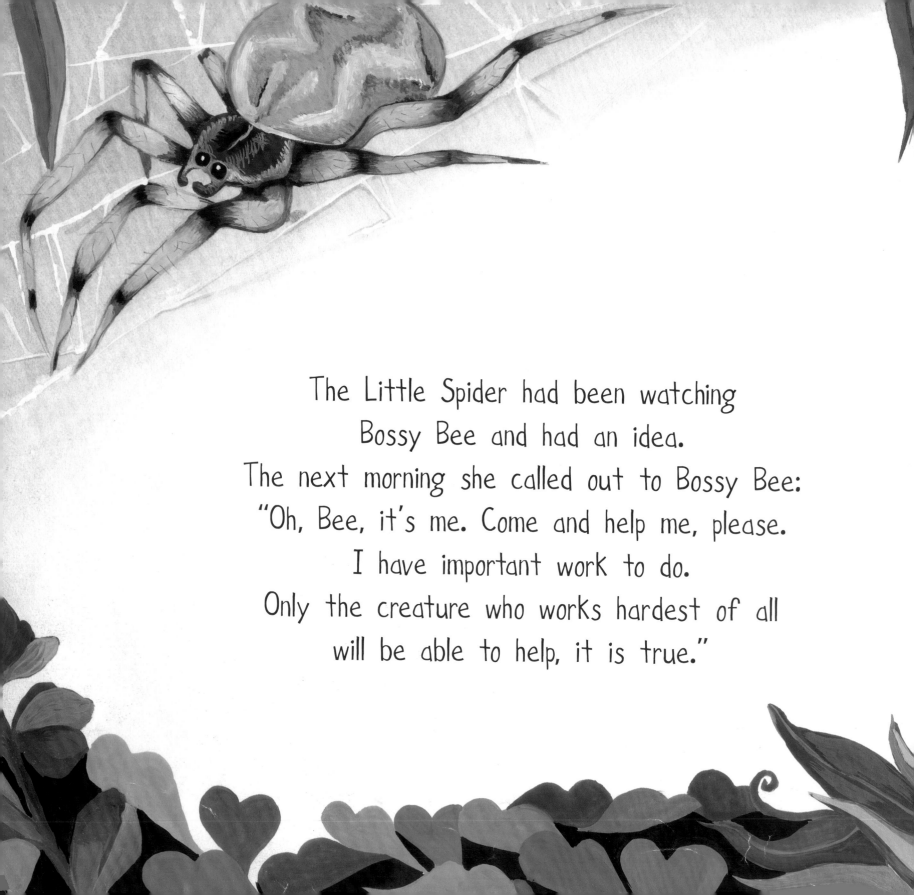

The Little Spider had been watching
Bossy Bee and had an idea.
The next morning she called out to Bossy Bee:
"Oh, Bee, it's me. Come and help me, please.
I have important work to do.
Only the creature who works hardest of all
will be able to help, it is true."

When the bee heard Little Spider's request, she
knew she was the one for the job.
"If there's important work to be done,
I will help Little Spider, you'll see.
Of all the creatures that live around here,
no one works as hard as a bee!"

And off she flew to see the Little Spider. But Little Spider had played a trick on Bossy Bee. As soon as the Bee landed on Spider's web, she was caught fast by the silvery thread. She couldn't move at all.

"Oh, Bossy Bee, you work so hard,
now it's your turn to rest.
Stop bossing the others and watch carefully.
You'll soon see what each creature does best."

All day long Bossy Bee was trapped. And
all day long she watched the other garden
creatures, busy at their work.
First, she noticed the earthworm.

"I'm a shy little worm. I stay underground.
I work out of sight, it is true.
I wriggle along to aerate the soil,
and fertilise it with my poo!"

Then she spotted the ladybug.
"My red and black wings may seem pretty and fine,
but I am helpful too.
When the aphids arrive to nibble the lettuce,
I gobble them up for you!"

Finally, the lizard appeared.
"I sleep a lot in the warm summer sun,
but I help in the garden too.
When slithery slugs come to ruin the crops,
I munch them all up — they're my food!"

Bossy Bee couldn't believe her eyes.
Never before had she noticed how busy
the other creatures were.

"Oh, Spider, I promise to
stop being bossy.
I've learned a lesson today.
I'll respect other creatures
and value their jobs.
We should work as a team
every day!"

And from that day on, the Little Spider woke each morning to the sounds of:

Wiggle, wiggle, wiggle.
Flitter, flutter, flit.
Gobble, gobble, crunch.
Bizzz, buzzz, buzzz.

But never again did she hear "boss-boss-boss."

Starfish Bay® Children's Books
An imprint of Starfish Bay Publishing
www.starfishbaypublishing.com

BIZZ BUZZ BOSS

Text copyright © Natalie McKinnon, 2019
Illustrations copyright © Margaret Tolland, 2019
ISBN 978-1-76036-056-6
First Published 2019
Printed in China by Beijing Shangtang Print & Packaging Co., Ltd.
11 Tengren Road, Niulanshan Town, Shunyi District, Beijing, China

Sincere thanks to Elyse Williams from Starfish Bay Children's Books for her creative efforts in preparing this edition for publication.

Natalie McKinnon is an early childhood educator with over twenty years' teaching experience in Australia. Natalie also presents environmental workshops for pre-school and elementary audiences. Her workshops encourage children to understand where real food comes from and to develop an understanding of the relationship between their health and the environment.

Margaret Tolland is an artist from New Zealand, whose illustrations are packed with detail. Through her work, get closer to the habitats and lifestyles of the many species, both flora and fauna, that she explores with an eye on environmental education. With twenty years' experience in visual arts education and working in a gallery, Margaret now illustrates full-time. Although she had a fear of spiders, after painting them in detail, she now appreciates how amazing they are.